Nothing Happened

Bill Harley

Illustrations by Ann Miya

TRICYCLE PRESS
Berkeley, California

TRICYCLE PRESS
P. O. Box 7123
Berkeley, CA 94707

Book design by Tasha Hall

Library of Congress Cataloging-in-Publication Data

Harley, Bill, 1954–
      Nothing Happened / by Bill Harley.
            p.   cm.
      Summary: A little boy stays up all night to see what
happens in his house after his bedtime.
      ISBN 1-883672-09-0
      [1. Night—Fiction. 2. Dwellings—Fiction.]
      I. Title
PZ7.H22655No   1995
[E]—dc20   94–10266
                                                          CIP
                                                          AC

First Tricycle Press printing, 1995
Manufactured in Singapore

1 2 3 4 5 6 — 99 98 97 96 95

For my two boys, Noah and Dylan

Thanks to Kitty Flynn

—B. H.

For Dean, who helped make
Something Happen

—A. M.

"Nothing happens."

That's what Jack's mom and dad always said when he asked them what happened at night after he went to bed. Jack didn't like going to bed first, because he was sure something happened.

"Nothing happens, " his mother would say.

"Nothing happens," his father would say.

But his older brother Will would say, "*Everything* happens!"

"We have a party every night as soon as you go to bed. My friends come and Mom's friends come and Dad's friends come and even *your* friends come. And there's a secret party room in the basement behind the furnace where you're afraid to go where we keep the party food and games. Something happens and you're the only one who doesn't get to be there."

"Will is just teasing you," his mother would say. But Jack thought maybe Will was right, because sometimes he woke up at night and he heard people laughing and talking downstairs. Even Will was asleep then. Jack could see him sleeping with his mouth open. He thought Will looked stupid when he slept with his mouth open, but Jack couldn't tell him that because Will was bigger and might hit him.

One night, Jack woke up and heard noises downstairs. He got out of his bed and walked by Will's. He
looked down at his brother and whispered, "You look
stupid when you sleep with your mouth open." He
walked down the hall and stood at the top of the stairs.
"Mom..." he called.

"What?"

"What's happening?"

"Nothing's happening."

"Something's happening. Who's down there?"

"Go back to bed, Jack."

"Are you eating anything?"

And then Jack's dad said, "Get to bed, Jack.
I don't want to come up there."

"Then don't!" Jack grumbled to himself
as he walked back to his room.

Jack was *sure* something happened after he went to bed. And so the next day he decided he was going to find out what he was missing.

Jack planned. He found a flashlight in the kitchen drawer. He put it under his mattress. He found some comic books on his brother's bookshelf. He hid them under his pillow. He made crackers with peanut butter, put them in a plastic bag, and put them under his mattress, too. He was ready to stay up all night. He felt like an explorer in his own house.

That night at bedtime, Jack kept his socks on so he would be ready for the party. He brushed his teeth and climbed into bed. His father came into his room and said, "Do you want me to read to you?"

"No. I'm too tired," Jack yawned.

His father tucked him in and said goodnight. When his father went downstairs, Jack got out of bed and looked out his window to the front yard and the street below. Where were the people who were coming to the party? Would they bring presents? Which one of his friends got to stay up later than he did? Probably all of them.

He watched and waited. Nothing happened. He heard his brother come upstairs. He ran to his bed and threw himself under the covers.

"Hoooonkkkkk-shoooooo," Jack snored, pretending to be asleep.

Will said, "That's dumb. You're not asleep."

"Yes I am. Don't bother me."

"You can't be asleep and talk to me."

"You talk all the time in your sleep." Jack closed his eyes tighter.

He heard his brother get into bed. The table lamp turned off. He opened his eyes a little bit—he could see Will, and, after a while, he saw Will's mouth open. He looked stupid. He was asleep.

Jack got out of bed and waited. Nothing happened. He looked out the window. Nothing happened. He got out some of the crackers from under the mattress and ate them.

Still, nothing happened.

No doorbell. No cars pulling up. No friends. He was getting bored, when all of a sudden he heard footsteps coming up the stairs. His father's footsteps. He ran to his bed and pulled the covers up. He closed his eyes tight. His father was coming down the hall.

His father knew! His father knew that Jack was trying to stay up all night. What was he going to do? He heard his father come into the room. He heard his father's footsteps coming closer…closer. He felt his father sit on the bed. HIS FATHER KNEW!

And then, Jack felt his father lean over him and kiss him on the cheek. He heard his father say, "I love you, Jack."

Jack thought, "I didn't know he did that."

Then he felt his father get up off his bed. Jack opened his eyes and saw him walk over to Will's bed and lean over Will. His father gave Will a kiss, and Jack heard him say, "I love you, Will."

Jack heard his father in the bathroom. Jack heard his mother come upstairs. Jack heard his mother in the bathroom. Jack heard them talking on the other side of the wall. It sounded like mumbling.

Then the house was quiet. Jack had never heard it so quiet before. A car drove down the street.

Something was about to happen! He got out of bed and ran to the window. He saw the car drive by. He sat and waited.

Nothing happened. Maybe his parents had snuck downstairs. He got the flashlight out from underneath his mattress. He tiptoed past his brother's bed.

The hall light was on.
Jack crept down the hall. His
parent's door was open a little bit.
He tiptoed down the stairs. He sat
on the bottom stair.
Nothing happened.

Jack walked into the kitchen. The clock ticked. Nothing happened.

He opened the basement door and reached for the light. It was too high. He turned on the flashlight and went down the stairs. He tried to be quiet. Each stair made a big squeak.

There was the furnace.

Carefully, he walked closer and closer, looking for the door to the party room. There were cobwebs. There were shadows. It was hard to see.

Jack had to find out. He had to go *behind* the furnace. It was really dark. Jack put his hand on the basement wall and felt for the secret door.

There was a sound behind him!

RUMBLE RUMBLE CLANK CLANK!
Jack's mind raced—what was it? *What could it be?*

It was just the furnace coming on. Jack could feel his heart beating as he stood there.

Nothing happened.

He shone the flashlight up and down the basement wall. There was no secret party room. Jack thought about his brother Will.

Jack climbed out from behind the furnace and went back upstairs. He turned on the light in the kitchen and poured a bowl of his favorite cereal. He poured milk on it and ate it. When he got to the bottom of the bowl, there was more milk, so he put in more cereal, but then it needed more milk. He ate three bowls.

Jack looked at some leftover cereal still floating at the bottom of his bowl. They were little circles floating in the milk. They looked just like Will's mouth. How many little circles would fit in Will's mouth?

Will had a big mouth.

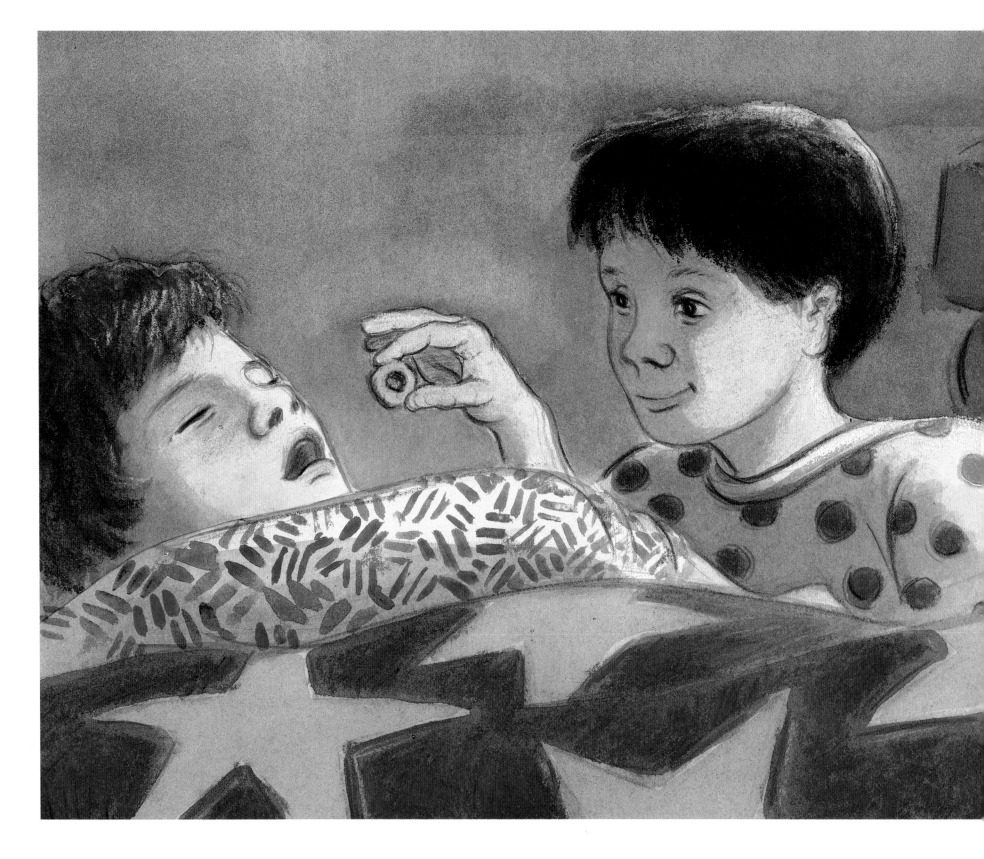

Jack filled two bowls with dry cereal and carried them upstairs. He tiptoed into his room. His brother was still sleeping. He took a piece of cereal and held it over Will's big, open mouth.

Jack stopped. Something might happen. He thought, "Will might choke."

He looked at Will's face. He liked how Will's nose went up a little at the end.

He dropped the piece of cereal back in the bowl and carried the bowls down to the kitchen. He put the cereal back in the box.

Jack sat in the living room and waited. Nothing happened. He sat in the dining room. Nothing happened. In the kitchen. On the back steps.

In the bathroom. (He didn't flush.) Nothing happened.

He read comic books and waited. And waited.

When was something going to happen? *Where* was the party?
   And then, something happened.

He saw it happen. He saw the sky slowly turn color. He saw the clouds turn bright pink, then gold.

Then, down at the far end of his street, he saw the sun rise.

It was morning. Jack went to his room. He could see his brother sleeping with his mouth open. He ran down the hall and into his parent's room. His dad was asleep. His mouth was open.

Jack had never noticed how much his father looked like Will. He leaned over and gave his dad a kiss on the cheek.

"I love you, Dad," he said. His dad opened one eye and looked at him.

"Guess what, Dad," Jack said.

"What?"

"I stayed up all night and guess what."

"What?"

"Nothing happened. Except the sun came up!"

His dad rolled over. Jack went downstairs.
He got out a new bowl and filled it with cereal.
He carried it back upstairs to his room and
climbed onto Will's bed. He held
the bowl over his brother's head
and called out, "Oh Wiiill!"
Jack tipped the bowl and
the cereal fell.

Will started to laugh.

"What's so funny?" asked Jack.

"Breakfast in bed!" Will said, and Jack laughed too. They sat on the bed and ate all the cereal.

From that day on Jack didn't worry about missing anything at night, because the night he stayed up, nothing happened.